THREE MASSES

Recent Researches in the Music of the Renaissance is one of four quarterly series (Middle Ages and Early Renaissance; Renaissance; Baroque Era; Classical Era) which make public the early music that is being brought to light in the course of current musicological research.

Each volume is devoted to works by a single composer or in a single genre of composition, chosen because of their potential interest to scholars and performers, and prepared for publication according to the standards that govern the making of all reliable historical editions.

Subscribers to this series, as well as patrons of subscribing institutions, are invited to apply for information about the "Copyright-Sharing Policy" of A-R Editions, Inc. under which the contents of this volume may be reproduced free of charge for performance use.

Correspondence should be addressed:

A-R Editions, Inc.
315 West Gorham Street
Madison, Wisconsin 53703

RECENT RESEARCHES IN THE MUSIC OF THE RENAISSANCE • VOLUME XXXI

Sebastian de Vivanco

THREE MASSES

Edited by Enrique Alberto Arias

A-R EDITIONS, INC. • MADISON

Copyright © 1978, A-R Editions, Inc.

ISSN 0486-123X

ISBN 0-89579-109-9

Library of Congress Cataloging in Publication Data:

Vivanco, Sebastián de, ca. 1550-1622.
  Three Masses.

  (Recent researches in the music of the Renaissance ;
v. 31)
  Includes bibliographical references.
  CONTENTS: Misa sexti toni.—Misa O quam suavis es.—
Missa Beata Maria Virgine in Sabbato.
  1. Masses—Vocal scores. I. Arias, Enrique Alberto.
II. Series.
M2.R2384   vol. 31   [M2011]   780'.903'1s   [783.2'2'54]
ISBN 0-89579-109-9   78-10386

Contents

Preface

The Composer

Among the native composers who never left the Iberian peninsula, Sebastian de Vivanco held a position of considerable importance.[1] The known facts of Vivanco's biography are few.[2] He was born around 1550 in Avila in north-central Spain, a city that had the distinction of being the birthplace of St. Theresa of Avila, St. John of God, St. Ignatius of Loyola, and Tomas Luis de Victoria. We know nothing of Vivanco's early years and education. The earliest extant information regarding him is dated July 4, 1576, when he was removed from the chapter at Lerida "for causes not to reflect on his honor."[3] He apparently served for a while as choirmaster in the Cathedral at Segovia, for a capitular act dated July 8, 1587, states that Vivanco had been in that post and that Hernando de Ysassi (the choirmaster replaced by Vivanco) was "old and tired and does not heed the requirements of his office."[4]

On August 7, 1587, Vivanco returned to Avila to become choirmaster there, with a monthly stipend of 4000 *maravedis*. Despite the offers made by the chapel at Seville, he remained at Avila where, on February 1, 1588, a large honorarium was voted him by the chapel. The same day he received this gift, Vivanco asked for a month's leave to visit Seville. Vivanco probably protracted this leave in order to assume the position of choirmaster at the Cathedral in Seville.

Once Vivanco arrived at Seville the "six regular boys" or *Los Seises* (a special group of choristers at the Cathedral) were transferred to him from Francisco Guerrero.[5] The one boy that Vivanco had brought with him from Avila (the dean of the Cathedral in Seville, Don Alonso de Rebenga, had asked for three) returned home. On March 17, 1588, the chapter of the Cathedral in Seville granted a final 100 ducats with which the composer returned to his original position at Avila. Why Vivanco did not stay in the prestigious position of choirmaster at Seville is unknown. Possibly, Vivanco may not have found things to his liking and decided to return to his more familiar Avila.

Vivanco remained at Avila until October 2, 1602, when he accepted a position as chapelmaster at Salamanca, where he was to remain for the rest of his life. On February 19, 1603, he acceded to the famous Chair of Music at the University of Salamanca, one of the highest possible honors given a Spanish musician.[6] That this was, indeed, an honor is proved by the fact that the Chair was held previously by no less a figure than Francisco de Salinas.[7] Vivanco remained as "morning professor" until January 9, 1621, when he retired. He died on October 26, 1622.[8]

The preface to Vivanco's book of Magnificats, the *Liber Magnificarum* (1607), reveals that Vivanco was in Holy Orders:

> Thou hast led me, O Holy Way,
> to the height of priesthood;
> Thou, O Spouse, hast not
> wished me to be in the lowest
> place in the house of Thy church,
> Thy spouse, but hast put me
> in charge of singers who daily
> sing divine praises to Thee,
> Highest Father, and to the
> Holy Spirit.[9]

Although little has been made of Vivanco's having been in Holy Orders, it may account for the fact that he led a quiet life rather than devoting himself to the seeking of higher offices; he was conspicuously absent from the courts of Phillip II and Phillip III.

The Masses[10]

Thirteen of Vivanco's Masses are extant: ten are complete; two, the *Missa Crux fidelis* and the *Misa In Manus Tuas*, are nearly complete; and one other, the *Missa Tu es vas electionis*, exists only as a fragment. Ten of these Masses were published in 1608 by the Flemish printer Artus Tabernelius. This print is now in the possession of the Archivo de Musica de la Capilla Real in Granada. The opening preface, the beginning section of the Kyrie, and three voices of the Christe to the *Missa Crux fidelis*, and large sections of the *Misa In Manus Tuas, a 8* (including the complete Credo as well as parts of the Gloria) are lost. This elaborate print, published at Salamanca,[11] was probably a compilation of works in honor of the positions Vivanco then held in that city.

Exact dates cannot be given for the Masses, but biographical information indicates that they must have been written during Vivanco's tenure at Segovia, Avila, and, finally, during the first few years at Salamanca—thus, the Masses were written during the last quarter of the sixteenth and the earliest part of the seventeenth centuries. The style of the

Misa Quarti Toni suggests that it is the earliest of all thirteen extant Masses.[12] The following are the ten settings of the Ordinary as found in the Granada print:

1. Page 5: *Missa Crux fidelis, a 6* (the opening Kyrie as well as three voices of the Christe are missing)
2. Page 34: *Misa Assumpsit Jesus, a 5*
3. Page 66: *Misa Doctor Bonus, a 4*
4. Page 88: *Missa Super Octos Tonos, a 4*
5. Page 112: *Misa O Quam suavis es, Domine, a 4*
6. Page 140: *Misa In Festo Beata Maria Virgine, a 4*
7. Page 168: *Missa Beata Maria Virgine in Sabbato, a 4*
8. Page 188: *Misa Quarti Toni, a 4*
9. Page 208: *Misa Sexti Toni, a 4*
10. Page 228: *Misa In Manus Tuas, a 8* (parts of the Gloria and all the Credo are missing)

Another source exists for four of these ten Masses. This print, now found at Valladolid (MS I), reduplicates the *Misa O Quam suavis es, Misa Doctor Bonus, Misa Sexti Toni,* and the *Misa Quarti Toni.* In the Valladolid MS, these four works are termed, respectively, *Misa Primi Toni, Misa Quinti Toni, Misa Sexti Toni,* and *Misa Quarti Toni.* The notation of pitch and rhythm is generally inaccurate in this manuscript. Also, this anthology was apparently intended for smaller, less sophisticated forces, since both the *Misa O Quam suavis es* and the *Misa Doctor Bonus* appear without their final elaborate Agnus Dei movements.

In 1974, two undated and unnamed manuscripts (for purposes of this discussion called MS I and MS II) were discovered at the *Real Monasterio de Nuestra Señora* at Guadalupe, Spain; they contain three previously unknown Masses as well as several motets ascribed to Vivanco.[13] The music in MS I and MS II seems to be from the earlier seventeenth century and was probably composed after Vivanco was teaching at Salamanca, since the ascriptions frequently refer to him as Magister. These manuscripts also contain works by Palestrina and Morales as well as music by lesser-known Spanish composers such as Navarro and Ribera.

The following is a listing of the works by Vivanco in these manuscripts as given in the order of the manuscripts' tables of contents:

MS I

Missa Tu es vas electionis, f. 139
(only the Kyrie and the opening of the Gloria are extant)

MS II

Missa de feria, a 4, f. 247
Kyrie—Sanctus--Motete: Petite et accepietis (in die letanie), f. 250—Agnus Dei
(f. 254 is missing)

Officium defunctorum, f. 255
Motete: Circumdederunt me, f. 273
Parce mihi, f. 261

Missa defunctorum, a 4, f. 264
De profundis, f. 277

Oficio de quaresma y semana santa
Miserere mei Secundi toni ad complet, *a 4,* f. 280
In manus tuas, *a 4,* f. 283
Vexilla Regis, *a 4,* f. 285
Arbor decora, *a 4,* f. 286
Motete: Ante diem, *a 4,* f. 291
Feria V in cena, *a 4,* f. 294 (Lamentatio)
Feria VI Lectio prima, *a 4,* f. 302
Sabbato Sancto, *a 4,* f. 307 (Lectio)
Motete: Christus factus est, *a 12,* f. 314

The ordering of contents and selection of texts in these manuscripts seem to have been governed by liturgical practice in and near Guadalupe. For example, the motet "Petite et accepietis" inserted in the *Missa de feria* uses a Proper text for Communion during Rogation days in spring. That the motet appears within a Mass without Gloria or Credo is indicative of an unusual liturgical practice that was perhaps a local custom. There is a tripartite division in the succession of works in MS II: (1) a short weekday Mass—the *Missa de feria*—including a Proper motet with the incipit "Petite et accepietis"; (2) an Office and Mass for the dead, again including several Proper motets; (3) and finally, a cycle of motets for Holy Week up to and including Holy Saturday.

The fragment of the *Missa Tu es vas electionis* shows similarity to the other Masses of Vivanco in its cantus firmus treatment (in long note values) of a particular melody; in this Mass, the melody remains unidentified. The *Missa de feria* and *Missa defunctorum* are, on the other hand, in a simple homophonic, syllabic style with the relevant Requiem chants in the highest voice of the latter work.

Melodic Sources for Works in This Edition

Surprisingly, none of Vivanco's Masses uses parody technique. Of the set of ten in the Tabernelius print, the *Misa Quarti Toni* and *Misa Sexti Toni* use no pre-existent material. The other eight Masses of the print are based on single melodic lines which in two instances (*Misa O Quam suavis es* and *Misa Assumpsit Jesus*) are drawn from the Superius parts of Vivanco's own motets on these texts. The two *Beata Maria Virgine* Masses use one of the succession of chants possible to such works during the sixteenth century.[14] The sources of the melodies for the *Missa Super Octos Tonos, Missa Crux fidelis,* and *Misa In Manus Tuas* have yet to be identified, though these may be hymns peculiar to a given locale in Spain.[15] All ten Masses in the Tabernelius print use the normal text disposition and placement of late sixteenth-century cyclic Masses. Characteristically, the *da nobis* portion of the Agnus is omitted, probably indicating a repeat performance of the first part of the Agnus Dei with the necessary change in text. The *Missa Beata Maria Virgine in Sabbato* lacks a Credo, perhaps again pointing to a local custom.

Unlike the two other Masses of this edition, which exhibit a variety of techniques in the use of pre-existent material, the *Misa Sexti Toni* is based on no pre-existent line; it is straightforward in its harmonic clarity, and is less demanding on the performers. It is shorter, simpler in melodic and contrapuntal style, and is without the complex polyphonic sections in more than four voices found in the other two Masses.

The *Misa O Quam suavis es* is a cantus firmus Mass, based on the Superius of Vivanco's own motet on the Antiphon text for first Vespers of Corpus Christi (L.U. 917).[16] The final portion of the Agnus Dei of this Mass calls for seven voices and uses the *O Quam suavis es* line in the highest part (labeled Superius II), as a cantus firmus treated in a strictly schematic manner.[17] Here the *O Quam suavis* melody is presented first beginning on A at m. 38, then on D at m. 56, after four measures of rest. At m. 70 the two-fold presentation of the melody is repeated exactly but in rhythmic diminution by one-half (indicated with the sign ₵ in the source). This kind of mathematical statement of a cantus firmus recalls the style of Obrecht.

The *Missa Beata Maria Virgine in Sabbato* uses the melodies of Kyrie IX, Gloria IX, Sanctus XVII, and Agnus Dei XVII, respectively, for each of its four movements. The Osanna is an elaborate movement making use of a four-in-one canon where three voices are derived from one (see Plate II). The print directs *Verte foliam et alteram videbis* or "Turn the page [page 182 of the Granada print] and you will see another [Osanna]." The question arises as to when one is to sing this alternate Osanna, since the previous musical section joins the text segments Benedictus and Osanna. The answer seems to be that this Osanna does not replace a previous section but acts as a possible addition, when a large, well-trained choir is performing. Furthermore, Vivanco used the additional Osanna to display his considerable compositional ability by deriving the three new voices from the Bassus part. The first derived voice appears two measures after the Bassus at m. 4 on d', the next begins at m. 9 on f', while the final entry occurs at m. 11 on c'' within a euphonious eight-voiced texture. Thus, although the voices are derived from the Bassus, they lie near the Superius in range. Both this section of the *Missa Beata Maria Virgine in Sabbato* and the final portion of the *Misa O Quam suavis es* are striking instances of Vivanco's contrapuntal virtuosity, as they have a complexity of style rare in the late sixteenth century.[18]

The Edition

The present edition is conservative in editorial matters. Barlines are regularly placed and are meant to act as visual coordinates. The measure is a convenient grouping of beats; but, especially in duple meter, it need not suggest an ensemble accent. Accent should be the result of the interaction between text phrasing, dissonance placement, and the general harmonic progression. Throughout, the reduction ◇ (semibreve) = ♩ prevails. Ligatures are indicated by ⌐‾‾⌐ (ligatures being almost without exception of the *cum opposita proprietate* variety), while coloration or hemiola cross-accent is indicated by ⌐ ‾⌐. In the triple-metered Osanna of the *Missa Beata Maria Virgine in Sabbato* the relationship to the previous duple section of ◇ = ◇ or the equivalent ♩ = ♩ has been used to give the proportional relationship implied in the measuration ₵ 3 as well as the proper feeling of rhythmic vitality. With the commencement of the *Benedictus,* the normal ◇ = ♩ returns.

The print is irregular in the matter of final fermatas, as it does not always place them over all of the voices at the end of a section. To be consistent, editorial fermatas are added in brackets [⌢] to all the voices originally without them. Furthermore, the note values themselves vary at the ends of sections; occasionally there are different values (such as ▭ and ⌐) in the various voices of a final chord. Accordingly, in a full measure in duple pulsation the final value in all the voices is given as ○ , while in a half-measure the final value is ♩ , regardless of the note values of the print.

The editor has adopted a conventional viewpoint regarding *musica ficta*. *Musica ficta* has most frequently been applied to achieve a semitone leading-tone cadence in those places where a momentary change of key-center seems implied. Only rarely was *musica ficta* needed to correct an augmented fourth or diminished fifth, since in most cases the Granada print itself supplies the necessary alterations. Performers are free, of course, to add to or disregard these accidentals as taste and knowledge require. Editorial accidentals are indicated within square brackets to facilitate performance; once they appear, they remain in effect throughout the measure in which they occur.

The Granada print handles text spelling, punctuation, and repetition in Renaissance fashion. The present editor has modernized these usages. Commas have been added for text repetition and the *Liber Usualis* (1956) has been used as a guide for hyphenation and spelling. Additional text underlay, resulting from *ij* text in the source, has been made by the editor; it appears within brackets. Unlike some Renaissance sources, the Granada print is quite accurate, clear, and helpful to both the scholar and performer in interpreting this music and text.

Performance Practice

The number of singers at the pontifical choir at Rome in the later sixteenth century may act as a guide to the usual disposition of forces at large liturgical establishments in the late Renaissance. After 1586 the full contingent of singers numbered twenty-one, thus suggesting that the present works are best performed by a small choir with four or five singers on a part.[19] Clarity of texture and rhythmic vitality are qualities of these works that should be emphasized in performance.

In Spanish cathedrals, as Stevenson has recently noted, doubling by instruments appears also to have been done.[20] In the present Masses doubling the long cantus firmus lines with a trombone or organ seems appropriate. In light of this suggestion, the Superius Secundus part has been placed above the final Agnus of the *Misa O Quam suavis es*. This last presentation of the cantus firmus strongly suggests either instrumental performance or doubling. In the full sections for four or more voices an occasional discreet doubling by winds or organ would conform with Spanish usage, though the sections for reduced parts imply *a capella* procedure.

Conclusion

In general, Vivanco's music is characterized by contrapuntal artifice, sensitive harmonic balance, and variety with an expressive use of augmented triads, frequent appearance of pre-existent melodies (rather than the pre-existent textures used in parody technique), and, in the Masses, a sense of expansiveness and large-scale unity. Our view of the Spanish Renaissance has been substantially widened because of the appearance of a representative number of Vivanco's sacred works in modern editions.

Enrique Alberto Arias
Chicago, Illinois

July 1978

Notes

1. For a discussion of the importance of the Flemish court of Phillip II see Gerard de Turnhout, *Sacred and Secular Songs for Three Voices*, ed. Lavern J. Wagner (Recent Researches in the Music of the Renaissance, vol. IX, A-R Editions, Inc., 1970), preface, and Ramon A. Pelinski, *Die Weltliche Vokalmusic Spaniens am Anfang Des 17. Jahrhundert: Der Cancionero Claudio de la Sablonara* (Tutzing: H. Schneider, 1971), pp. 78 ff.

2. There are several sources which virtually recapitulate the known facts regarding Vivanco's biography. Most notably, these are: Robert Stevenson, *Spanish Cathedral Music in the Golden Age* (Berkeley: University of California Press, 1961), pp. 247-78; also E.A. Arias, "The Masses of Sebastian de Vivanco (circa 1550-1622), A Study of Polyphonic Settings of the Ordinary" (Ph.D. diss., Northwestern University, 1971), pp. 5-14.

3. The entire notice is quoted by Higini Anglès, *Las Ensaladas de Mateo Flecha* (Barcelona, 1954), p. 25.

4. Stevenson, *Spanish Cathedral Music*, p. 275.

5. For the history of the *seises* see Gustave Reese, *Music in the Renaissance* (New York: W. W. Norton, 1959), pp. 596-7. One of the most striking functions of the *seises* (or six boys) was that these young choirboys were expected to dance in a ceremonial fashion, particularly on Corpus Christi. The office of *Maestro* in charge of these boys was both an important duty and a mark of distinction.

6. Salamanca had an especially glorious history in Renaissance Spain and has the distinction of founding the first Chair in Music. See Nan Cooke Carpenter, *Music in Medieval and Renaissance Universities* (Norman: University of Oklahoma Press, 1958), pp. 211 ff.

7. Carpenter, *Music in Medieval and Renaissance Universities*, p. 214.

8. Montague Cantor in "The *Liber Magnificarum* of Sebastian de Vivanco" (Ph.D. diss., New York University, 1967), p. 7, argues that Vivanco may have been born in 1551, which would make 1621 an even anniversary year and a more likely age for retirement.

9. "Tu me, O Via Sancta, ad sacerdotii culmen duxisti; Tu, O Sponsa, in Ecclesiae sponsae tuae domo non infimo in loco esse voluisti, sed Cantoribus, qui Patri excelso tibi, et Spiritui Sancto quotidie laudes divinos decantant, me praefuisti." Cantor, "The *Liber Magnificarum*," vol. II: 11.

10. In addition to the Masses, there is a complete book of Vivanco Magnificats (1607) (see Cantor, "The *Liber Magnificarum*") as well as of a large collection of his motets (see Samuel Rubio, *Antologia polifonia sacra* [Madrid: Ed Coculsa, 1954 and 1956] and Arias, "The Masses," vol. II). In his book *Spanish Cathedral Music in the Golden Age*, Robert Stevenson has thoroughly analyzed several examples of both Magnificats and motets.

11. The colophon reads: "Salamanticae, Excudebat Artus Tabernelius Antverpianus, VIII Kalendas Octobris, MDCIIX."

12. Arias, "The Masses," pp. 43-4

13. I am grateful for the assistance of Dr. David Crawford of the University of Michigan who first discussed these sources at the Fall 1974 regional meeting of the American Musicological Society at Chicago. Certainly these MSS at the *Real Monasterio de nuestra Señora* hold importance for our understanding of local Spanish liturgical usage in this period. Dr. Crawford has published part of the results of his investigation in "Two Choirbooks of Renaissance Polyphony at the Monasterio de nuestra Señora of Guadalupe," *Fontes Artis Musicae* xxiv (1977/3): 145. There is a detailed discussion of the repertoire's relation to Salamanca and Toledo as well as of the history of the monastery, together with an important inventory of the sources.

14. See Nors S. Josephson, "The *Missa de Beata Virgine* of the Sixteenth Century" (Ph.D diss., University of California at Berkeley, 1970), which discusses the tradition of which these two Masses are a part and which gives numerous comparative tables throughout.

15. Arias, "The Masses," p. 27.

16. The Granada print gives this text as *O Quam suavis es*, rather than the *O Quam suavis est* of the *Liber Usualis*. Vivanco's motet from which the cantus firmus of this Mass is taken also has the text with *est*.

17. Arias, "The Masses," pp. 112 ff.

18. Stevenson, Cantor, and Arias in their respective works have made frequent reference to this outstanding characteristic of contrapuntal virtuosity.

19. Lewis Lockwood, "Notes on the Text and Structure of the Pope Marcellus Mass," in his *Norton Critical Scores* edition of Palestrina's Mass by this name (New York: W. W. Norton, 1975), pp. 78-9.

20. Robert Stevenson, in "The First New World Composers," *JAMS*, xxxii (Spring 1970): 97, says, "During Olaso's two decades (1544-63) Segovia cathedral music constantly involved professional shawmers, sackbuts, and other instrumentalists, usually hired with two-year contracts."

Plate I. *Misa O Quam suavis es*, beginning of the final Agnus Dei:
from the 1608 Tabernelius print of Vivanco's Masses.
(Held by the Archivo de Musica de la Capilla Real, Granada)

Plate II. *Missa Beata Maria Virgine in Sabbato*, the alternate Osanna
including the Bassus part (p. 183): from the 1608 Tabernelius print of Vivanco's Masses.
(Held by the Archivo de Musica de la Capilla Real, Granada)

THREE MASSES

Misa Sexti Toni

Kyrie

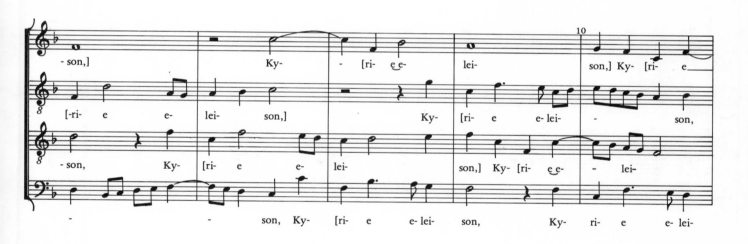

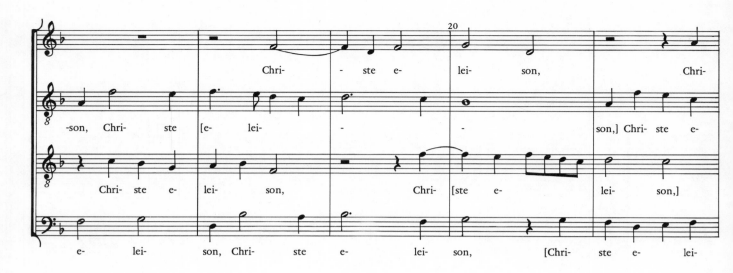

Gloria

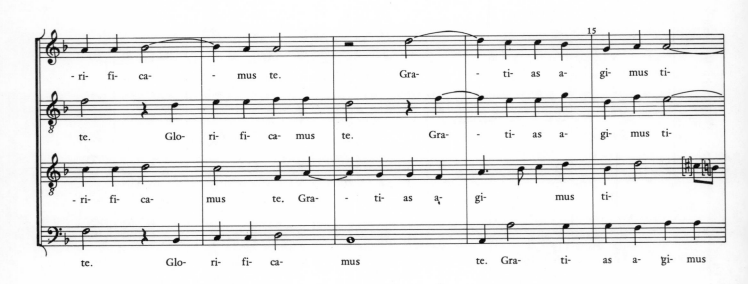

5

Do- mi- nus. Tu so- lus Al- tis- si- mus, Je- su

Do- mi- nus. Tu so- lus Al- tis- si- mus, Je- su

so- lus Do- mi- nus. Tu so- lus Al- tis- si- mus, Je- su Chri-

-nus. Tu so- lus Al- tis- si- mus, Je- - su Chri-

Chri- ste. Cum Sancto Spi- ri- tu, in glo- ri- a De-

Chri- ste. Cum Sancto Spi- ri- tu, in

-ste. Cum Sancto Spi- ri- tu, in glo- ri- a De- i

-ste. Cum Sancto Spi- ri- tu, in glo- ri-

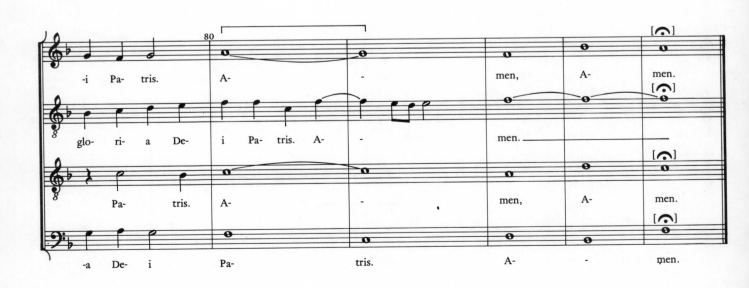

-i Pa- tris. A- men, A- men.

glo- ri- a De- i Pa- tris. A- men.

Pa- tris. A- men, A- men.

-a De- i Pa- tris. A- men.

Credo

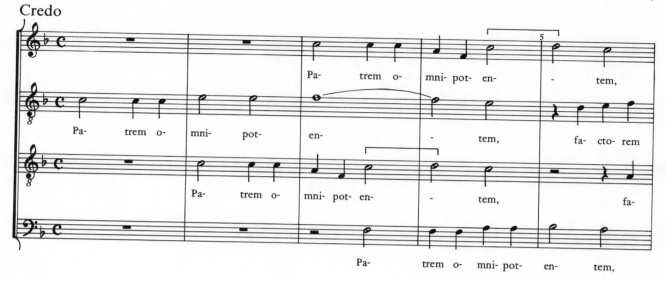

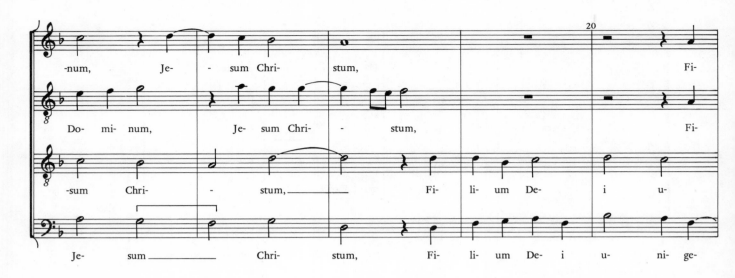

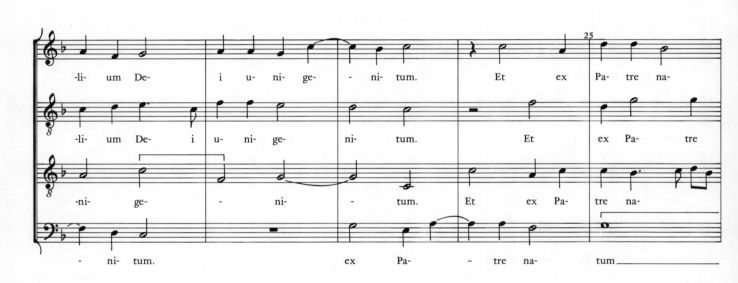

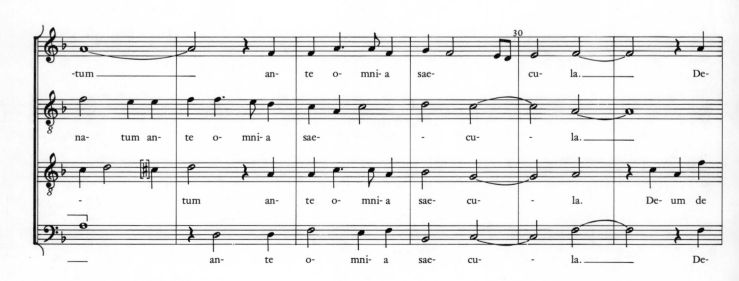

12

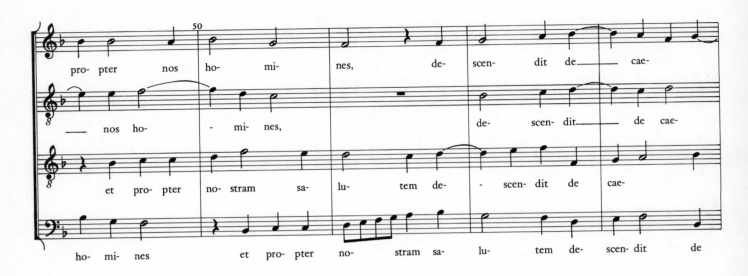

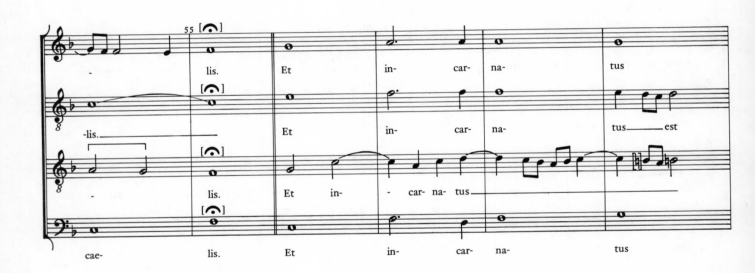

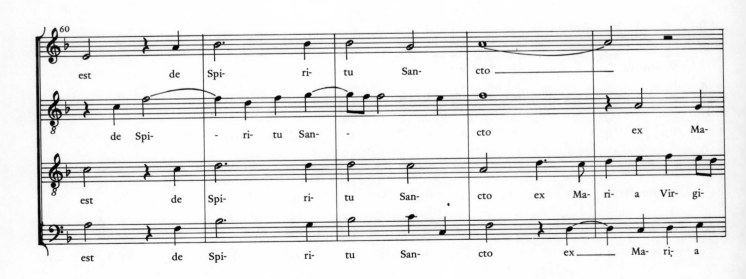

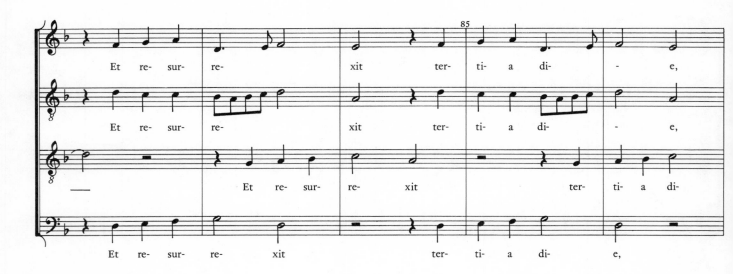

Et re- sur- re- xit ter- ti- a di- e,

Et re- sur- re- xit ter- ti- a di- e,

Et re- sur- re- xit ter- ti- a di-

Et re- sur- re- xit ter- ti- a di- e,

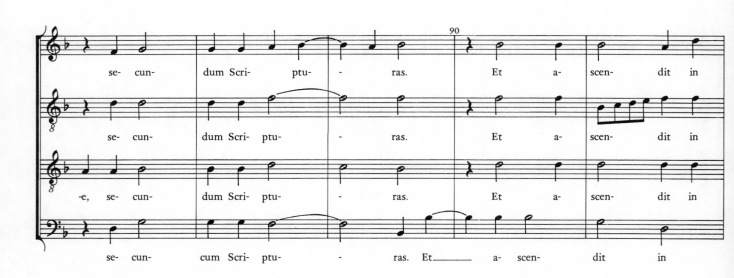

se- cun- dum Scri- ptu- ras. Et a- scen- dit in

se- cun- dum Scri- ptu- ras. Et a- scen- dit in

-e, se- cun- dum Scri- ptu- ras. Et a- scen- dit in

se- cun- cum Scri- ptu- ras. Et a- scen- dit in

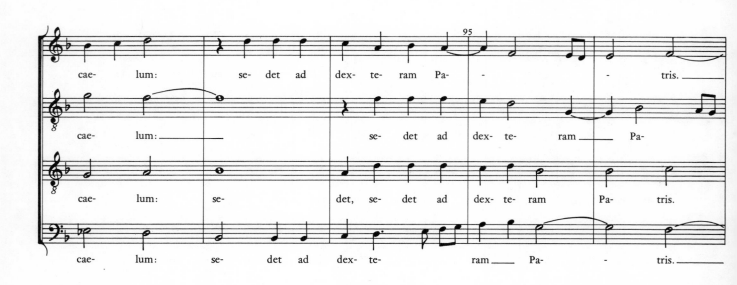

cae- lum: se- det ad dex- te- ram Pa- tris.

cae- lum: se- det ad dex- te- ram Pa-

cae- lum: se- det, se- det ad dex- te- ram Pa- tris.

cae- lum: se- det ad dex- te- ram Pa- tris.

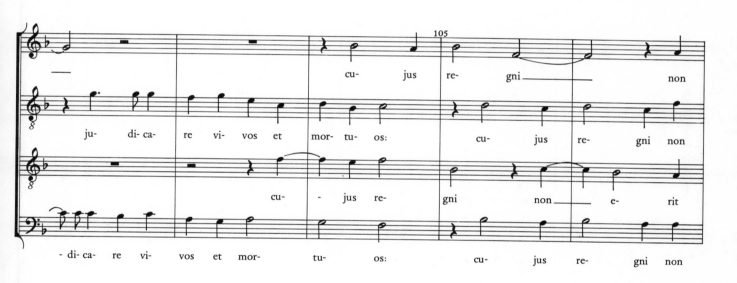

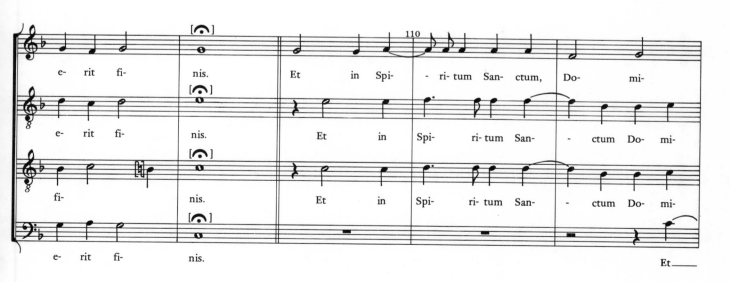

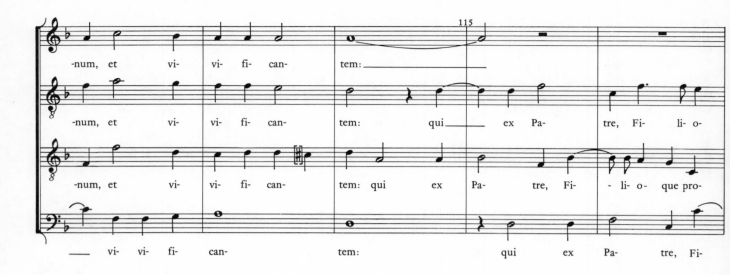

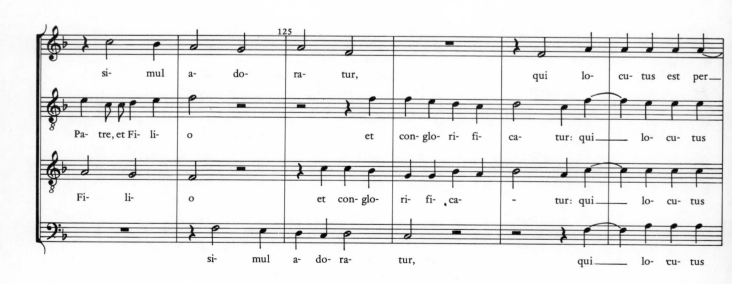

17

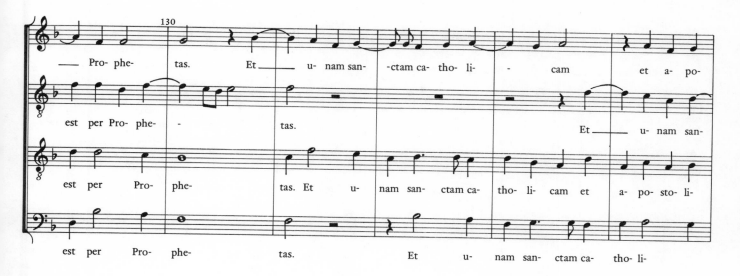

18

rum. Et ex- spe- cto re- sur- re- cti- o- nem mor-

rum. Et ex- spe- cto re- sur- re- cti- o- nem mor-

rum. Et ex- spe- cto re- sur- re- cti- o- nem mor-

rum. Et ex- spe- cto re- sur- re- cti- o-

-tu- o- rum. Et vi- tam, Et vi- tam,

-tu- o- rum. Et vi- tam, Et vi- tam ven- tu- ri

-tu- o- rum. Et vi- tam, Et vi- tam, Et vi- tam ven-

- nem mor- tu- o- rum. Et vi- tam, Et vi-

Et vi- tam ven- tu- ri sae- cu- li. A- men.

sae- cu- li, et vi- tam ven- tu- ri sae- cu- li. A- men.

-tu- ri sae- cu- li. A- men, A- men.

-tam ven- tu- ri sae- cu- li. A- men, A- men.

Sanctus

20

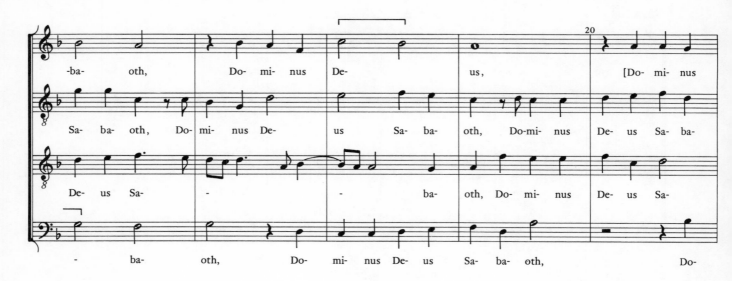

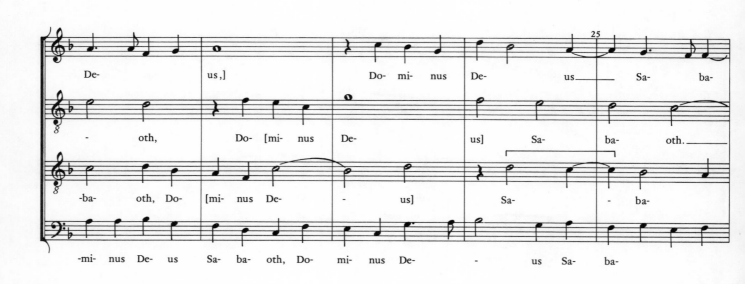

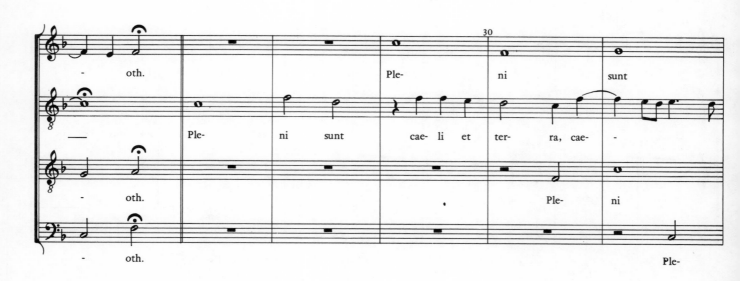

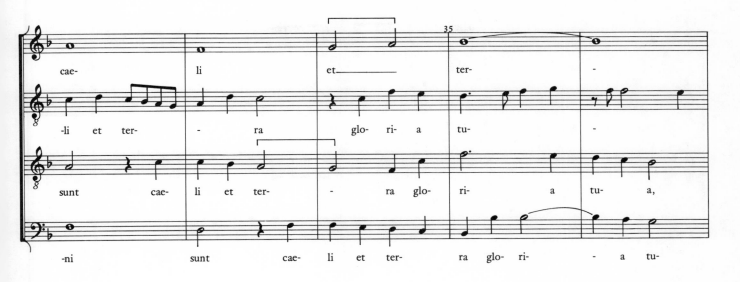

-ni. Ho- san- na in ex-cel- sis, Ho- san- na in ex- cel-

Do- mi- ni.____ Ho- san- na in ex- -cel- sis, Ho-

-mi- ni.____ Ho- san- na in ex- cel- sis, Ho- san- na in ex-

Ho- san- na in ex- cel- sis, in ex- cel- sis, Ho- san- na

-sis, Ho- [san- na in ex- cel- -sis.]

[-san- na in ex- cel- sis, Ho- san- na in ex- cel- -sis.]

-cel- -sis, Ho- san- na in ex- cel- sis.

in ex- cel- -sis, Ho- san- na in ex- cel- -sis.

Agnus Dei

A- -gnus____

A- gnus De- -

A- gnus De- -

Misa O Quam suavis es

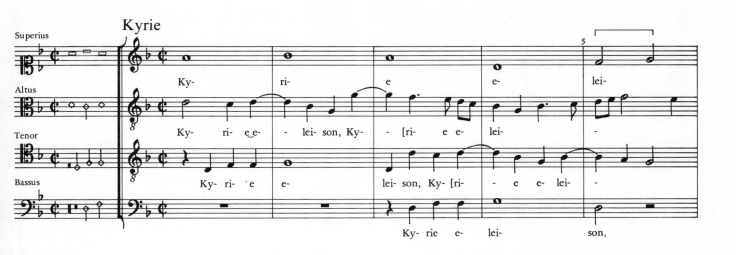

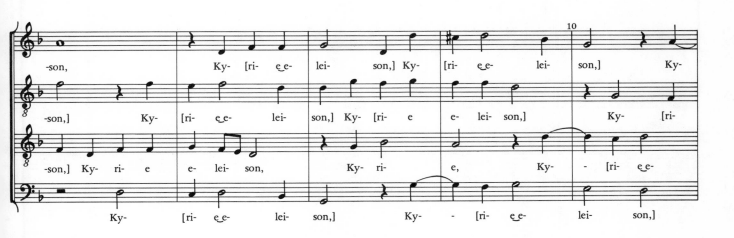

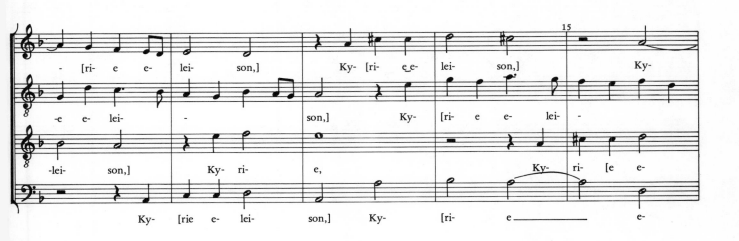

28

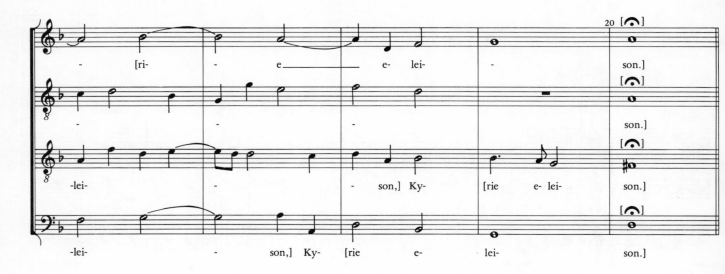

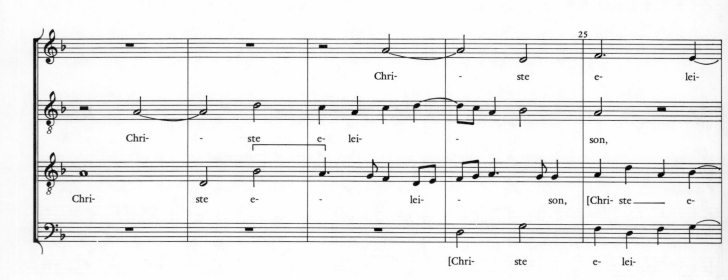

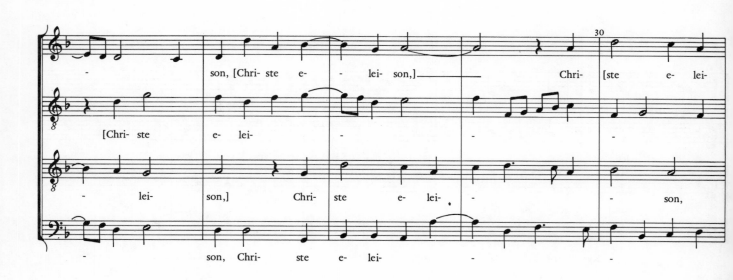

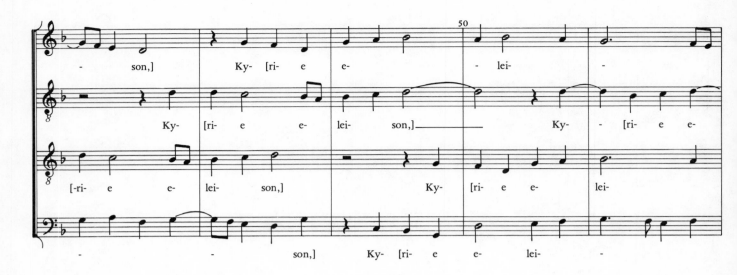

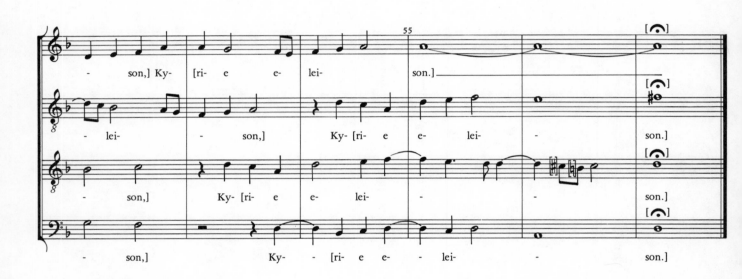

Gloria

-as a- gi- mus ti - bi _____ pro-

-as a- gi- mus ti- bi pro- -pter ma- gnam glo- ri- am

-as a- gi- mus ti- bi pro- -pter

_____ a- gi- mus ti - bi pro- pter,

-pter ma- gnam glo- ri- am _____ tu - - - am.

tu- am, glo- ri - am _____ tu - - am.

ma- gnam glo- ri- am tu- am, pro- -pter ma- gnam glo- ri- am tu- am. Do-

pro- pter ma- gnam glo- ri- am tu - am. _____

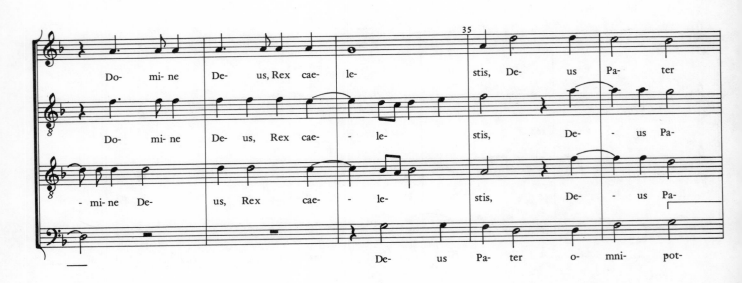

Do- mi- ne De- us, Rex cae- le- stis, De- us Pa- ter

Do- mi- ne De- us, Rex cae- le- stis, De- us Pa-

-mi- ne De- us, Rex cae- le- stis, De- us Pa-

De- us Pa- ter o- mni- pot-

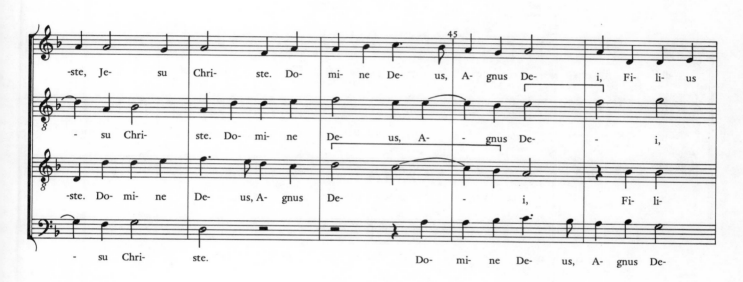

mun- di, mi- se- re- re no- bis. Qui tol- lis pec- ca- ta mun-

mun- di, mi- se- re re no- bis. Qui tol- lis pec- ca- ta mun-

- di, mi- se- re- re no- bis. Qui tol- lis pec- ca- ta mun-

mun- di, mi- se- re- re no- bis.

-di, sus- ci- pe de- pre- ca- ti- o- nem no- stram.

-di, sus- ci- pe de- pre- ca- ti- o- nem no-

-di, sus- ci- pe de- pre- ca- ti- o- nem no-

sus- ci- pe de- pre- ca- ti- o- nem no- stram.

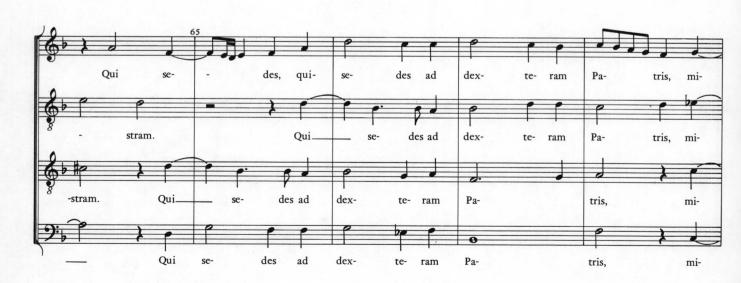

Qui se- des, qui se- des ad dex- te- ram Pa- tris, mi-

- stram. Qui se- des ad dex- te- ram Pa- tris, mi-

-stram. Qui se- des ad dex- te- ram Pa- tris, mi-

Qui se- des ad dex- te- ram Pa- tris, mi-

in glo- ri- a De- i Pa- tris. A- - men.
-a De- i Pa-tris, De- i Pa- tris. A- - men.
-a, in glo- ri- a De- i Pa- tris. A- - men.
-a De- i Pa- - tris. A- men. De- i Pa- tris. A- - men.

Credo

fa- cto- rem cae-
Pa- trem o- mni- pot- en- tem, fa- cto- rem cae- li ___ et ter-
Pa- trem o- mni- pot- en- tem, fa- cto- rem cae- li et ter- rae, vi-
fa- cto- rem cae-

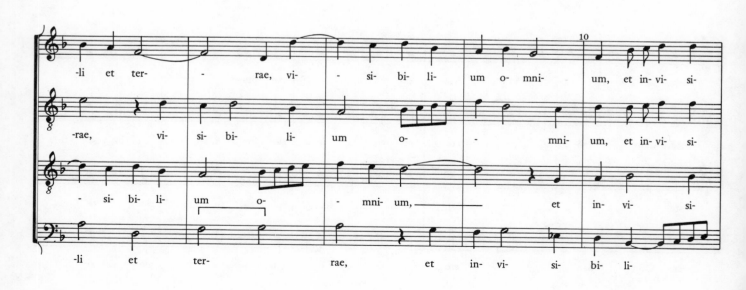

-li et ter- - rae, vi- - si- bi- li- um o- mni- um, et in- vi- si-
-rae, vi- si- bi- li- um o- - mni- um, et in- vi- si-
-si- bi- li- um o- - mni- um, ___ et in- vi- si-
-li et ter- - rae, et in- vi- si- bi- li-

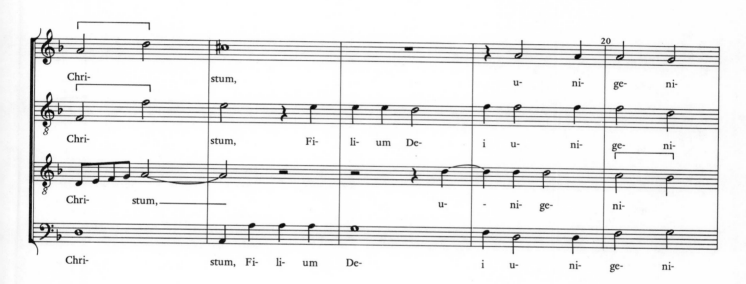

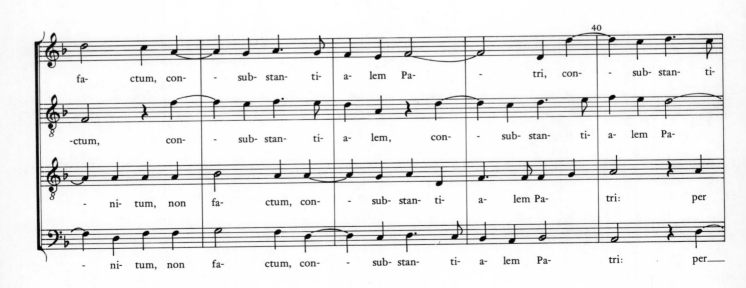

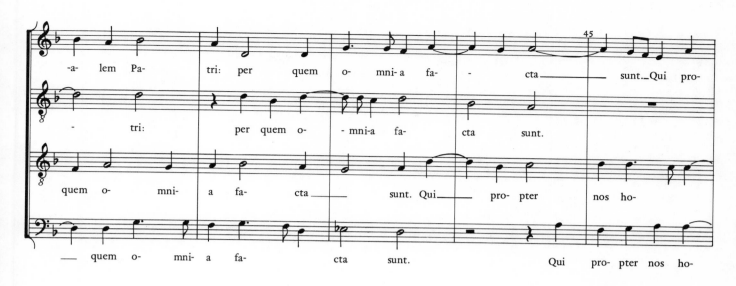

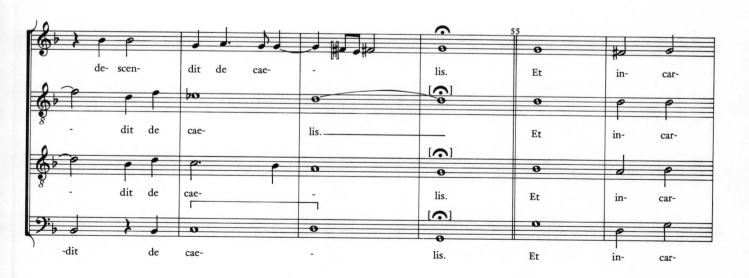

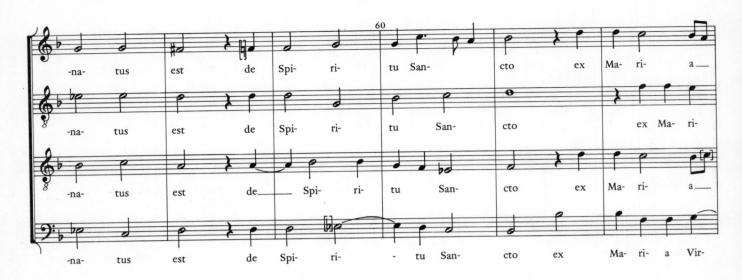

-na- tus est de Spi- ri- tu San- cto ex Ma- ri- a

-na- tus est de Spi- ri- tu San- cto ex Ma- ri-

-na- tus est de Spi- ri- tu San- cto ex Ma- ri- a

-na- tus est de Spi- ri- tu San- cto ex Ma- ri- a Vir-

Vir- gi- ne: Et ho- mo fa- ctus est.

-a Vir- gi- ne: Et ho- mo fa- ctus est.

Vir- gi- ne: Et ho- mo fa- ctus est.

- gi- ne: Et ho- mo fa- ctus est.

sub Pon- ti- o Pi- la-

sub Pon- ti- o Pi- la-

Cru- ci- fi- xus et- i- am pro no- bis:

Cru- ci- fi- xus et- i- am pro no- bis:

-to pas- sus, et se- pul- tus est. ter- ti- a

-to pas- sus, et se- pul- tus est. Et re- sur- re- xit ter-

pas- sus, et se- pul- tus est. Et re- sur- re-

pas- sus, et se- pul- tus est. ter-

di- e, se- cun- dum Scri- ptu- -

-ti- a di- e, se- cun- dum Scri- ptu- - ras.

-xit ter- ti- a di- e, se- cun- dum Scri- ptu-

-ti- a di- e, se- cun- dum Scri- ptu- ras. Et

-ras. Et a- scen- dit in cae- lum:

Et a- scen- dit in cae- lum: se- det ad dex-

-ras. Et a- scen- dit in cae- lum: Et a- scen- dit in

a- scen- dit in cae- lum: Et

*Bb in source.

mor- tu- os: cu- jus re- gni non e- rit fi - nis.

mor- tu- os: cu- jus re- gni non e- rit fi - nis.

mor- tu- os: cu- jus re - gni non e- rit fi - nis.

mor- tu- os: cu- jus re- gni non e- rit fi - nis.

Et in Spi- ri- tum San- ctum, Do- mi- num, et vi- vi- fi-

Et in Spi- ri-tum San- ctum, Do- mi- num, et vi- vi- fi-

Et in Spi- ri- tum San- ctum, Do- mi- num, et

Et in Spi- ri-tum San- ctum, Do- mi- num, et

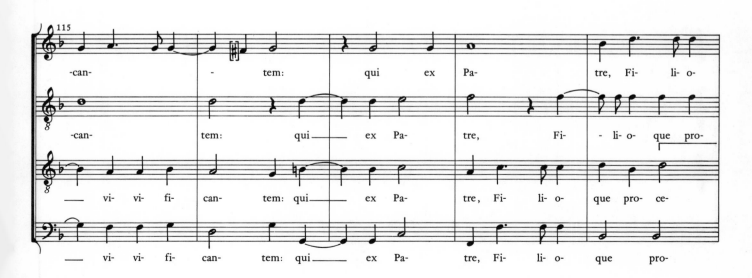

-can- tem: qui ex Pa- tre, Fi- li- o-

-can- tem: qui ex Pa- tre, Fi- li- o- que pro-

vi- vi- fi- can- tem: qui ex Pa- tre, Fi- li- o- que pro- ce-

vi- vi- fi- can- tem: qui ex Pa- tre, Fi- li- o- que pro-

44

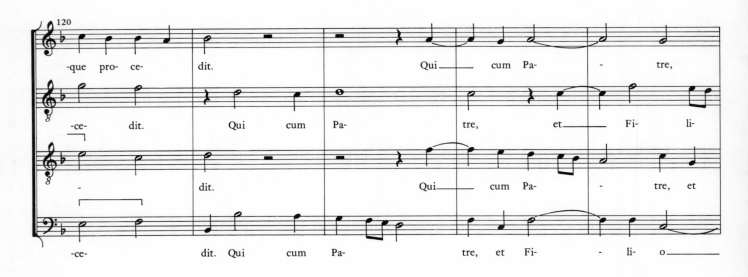

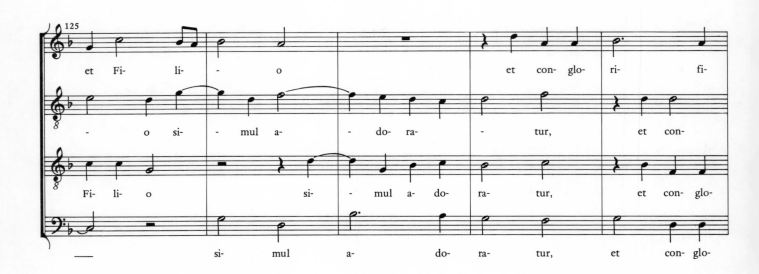

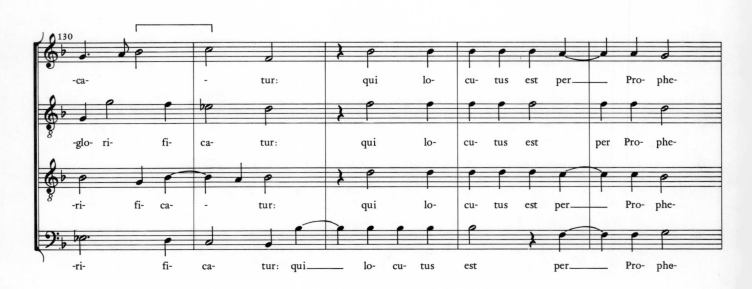

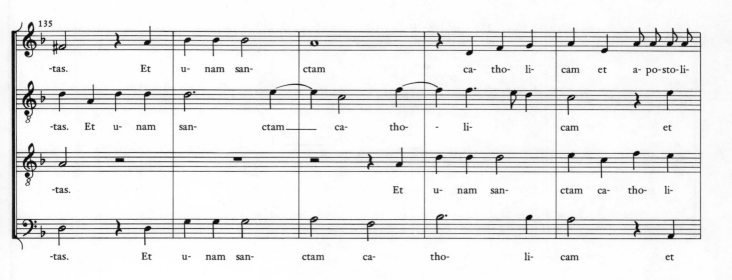

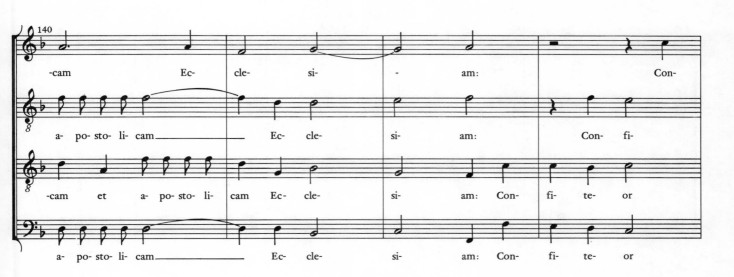

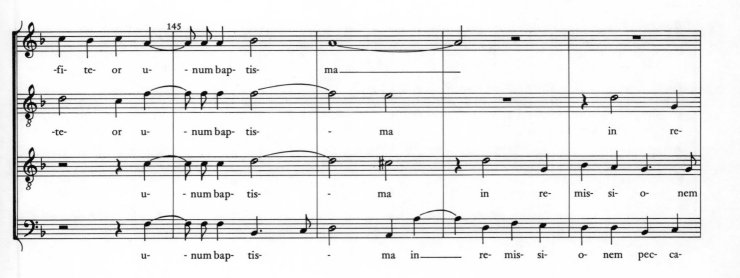

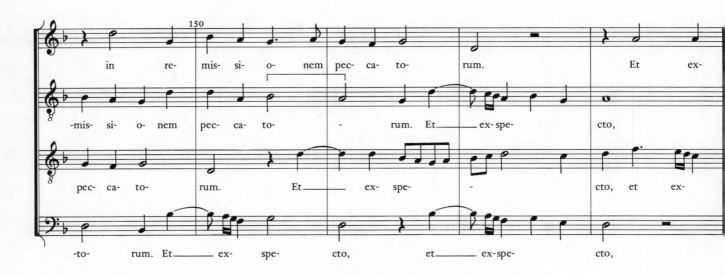

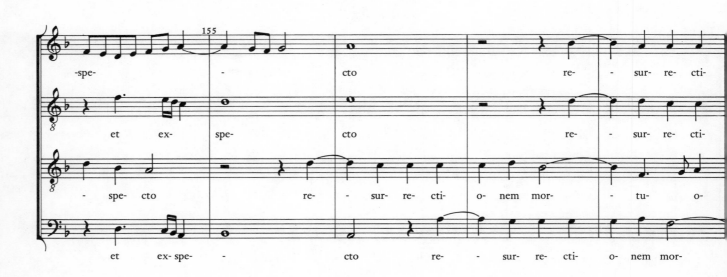

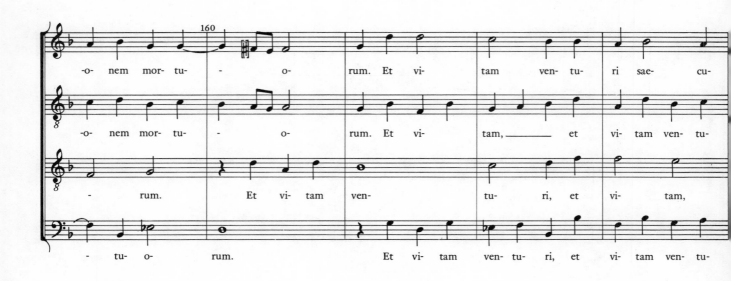

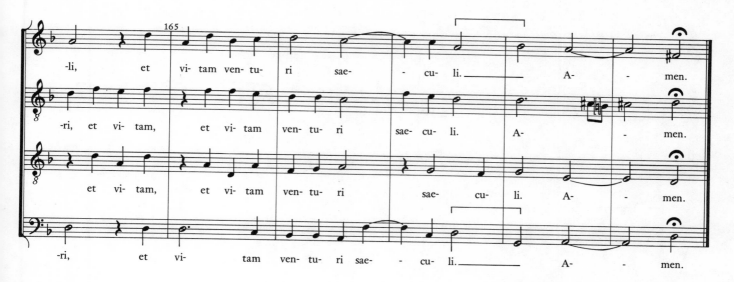

-li, et vi- tam ven-tu- ri sae - cu- li. A- men.

-ri, et vi- tam, et vi- tam ven-tu- ri sae-cu- li. A- men.

et vi- tam, et vi- tam ven-tu- ri sae- cu- li. A- men.

-ri, et vi- tam ven-tu- ri sae - cu- li. A- men.

Sanctus

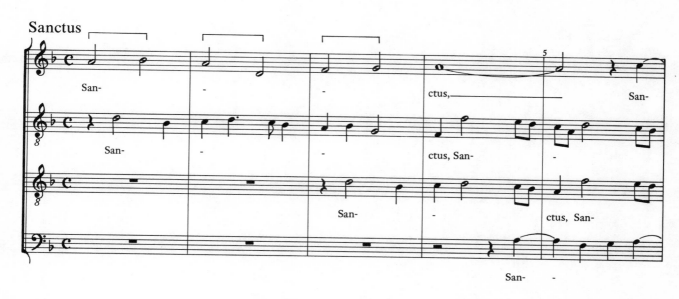

San- ctus, San-

San- ctus, San-

San- ctus, San-

San- -

-ctus, San- ctus, San- ctus, San-

-ctus, San- ctus, San-

- -ctus, San- San- ctus, San-

- - ctus, San- ctus,

48

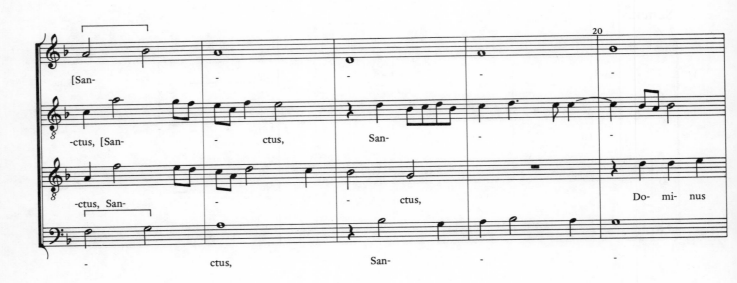

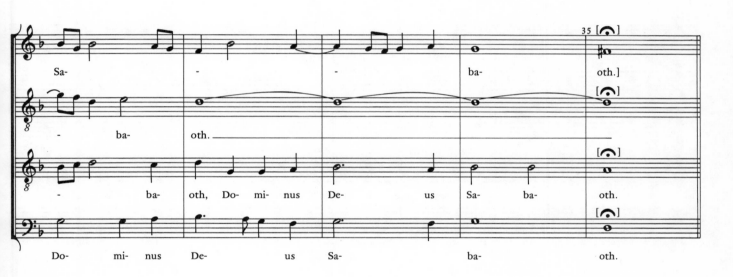

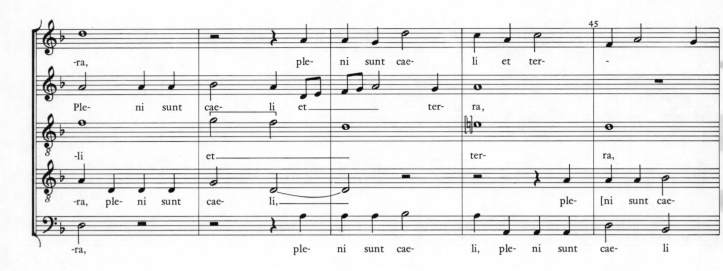

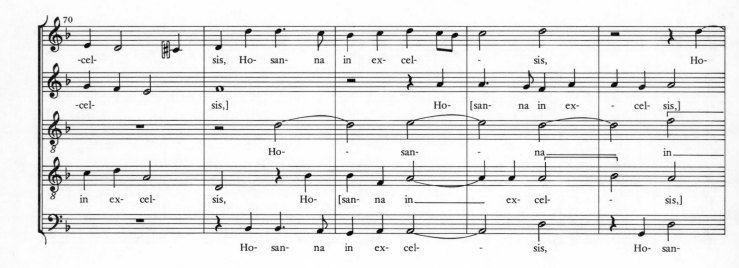

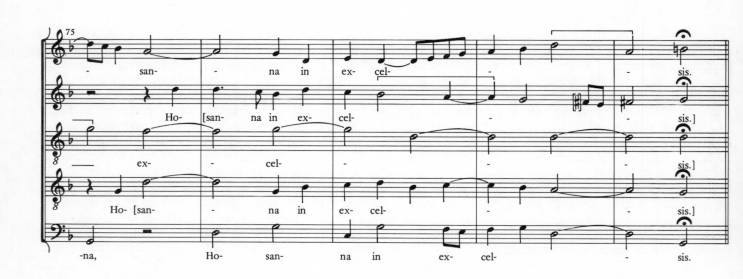

54

Agnus Dei

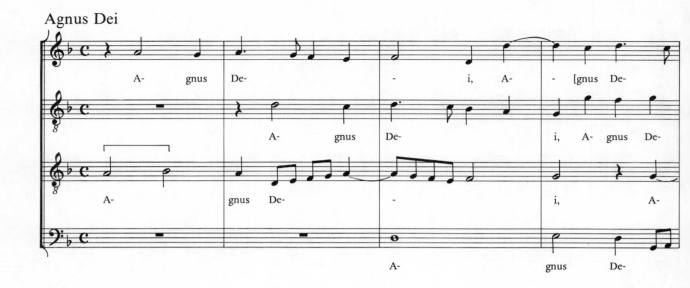

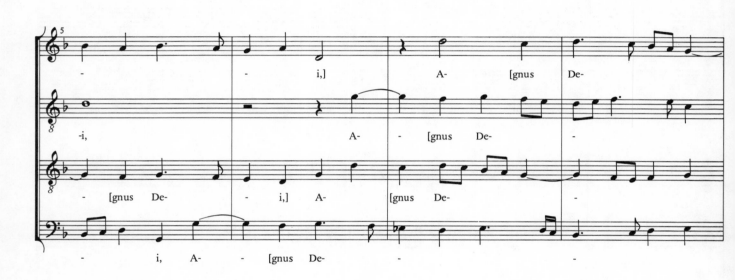

Missa Beata Maria Virgine in Sabbato

63

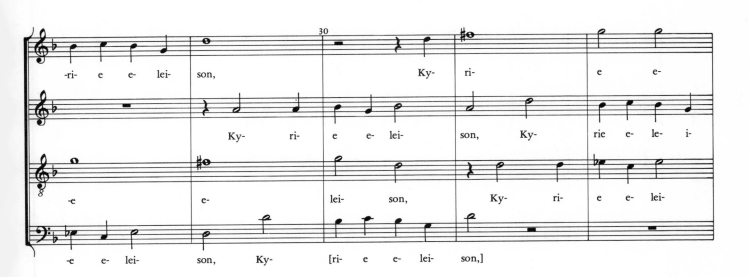

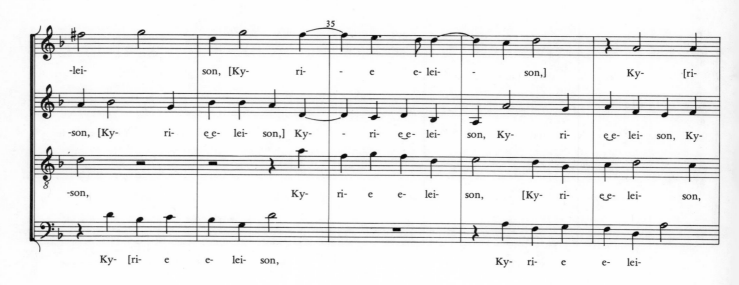

Gloria

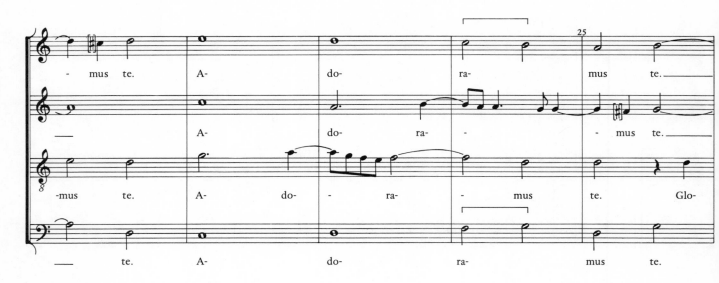

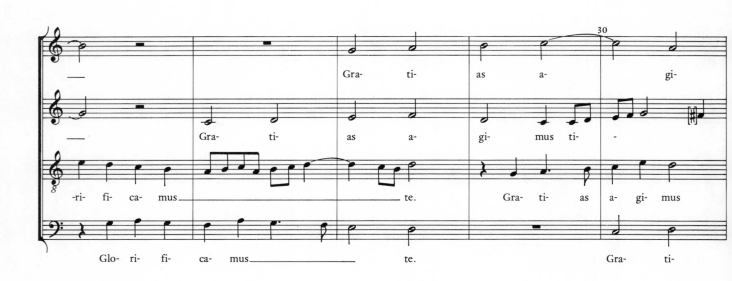

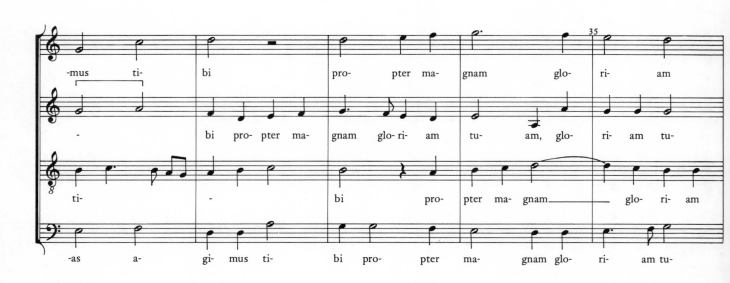

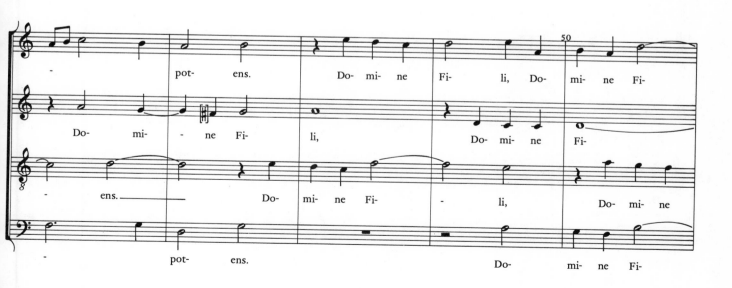

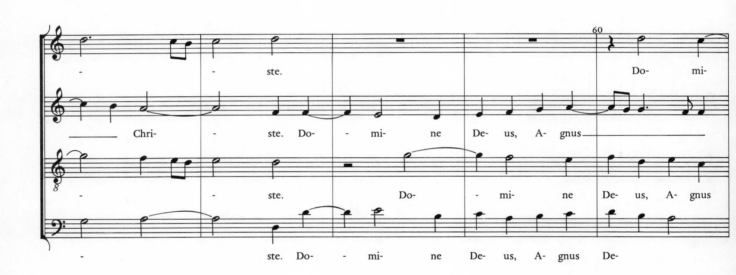

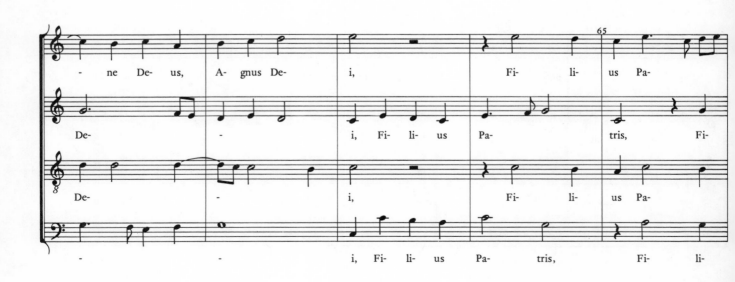

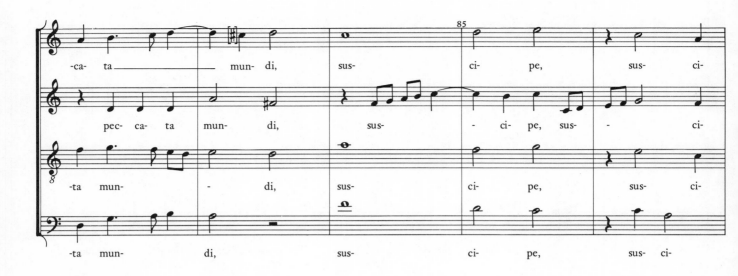

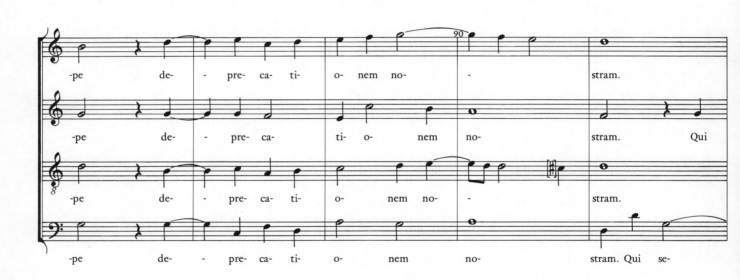

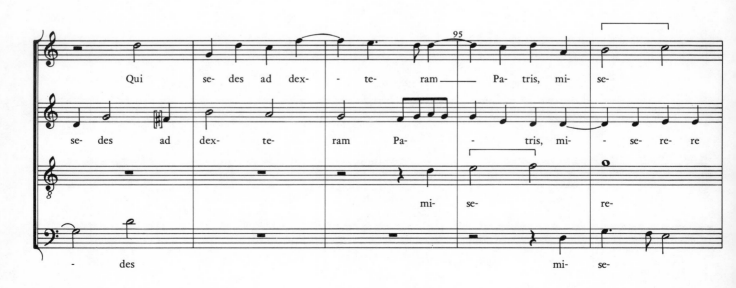

glo- ri- a De- i Pa- tris. A- - - men.

in glo- ri- a De- i Pa- tris. A- men.

-i, in glo- ri- a De- i Pa- tris. A- - men.

- ri- a De- i Pa- tris. A- - - men.

Sanctus

San- - - -

San- - -

San- - - ctus, [San- - - ctus,]

San-

-ctus, San- - - -

-ctus, San- - -

-ctus, [San- - - - ctus, San- -

San- - ctus, San- -

- - - ctus, [San- - -

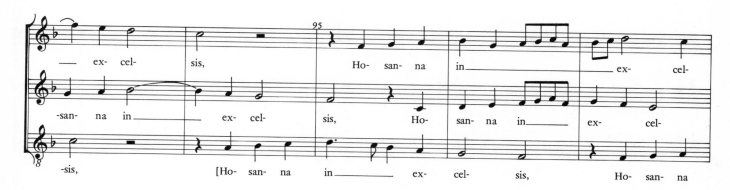

Superius *Verte foliam et alteram videbis.*

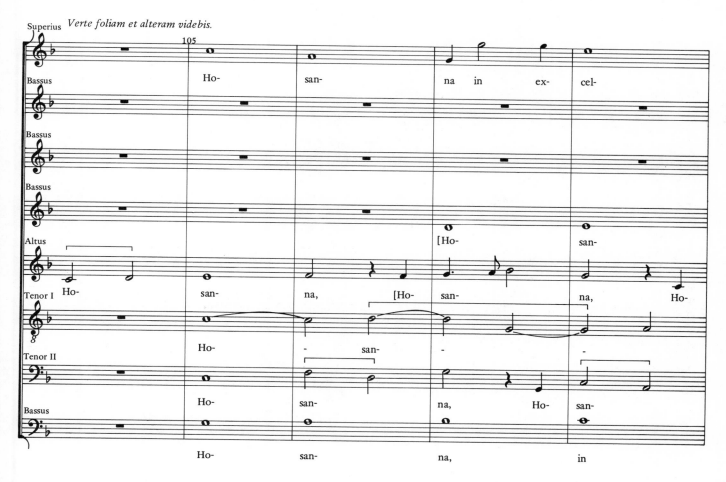

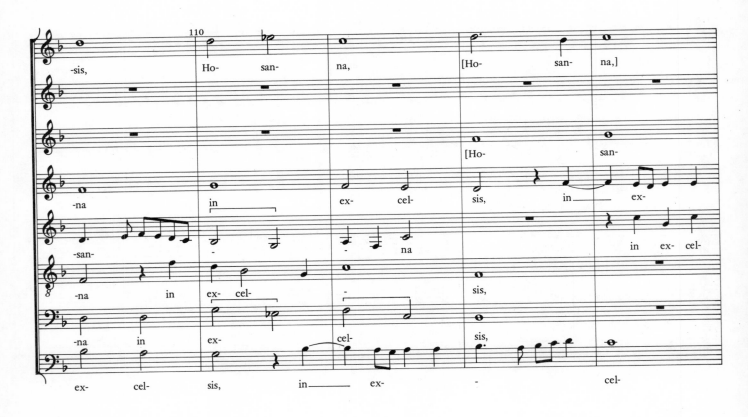

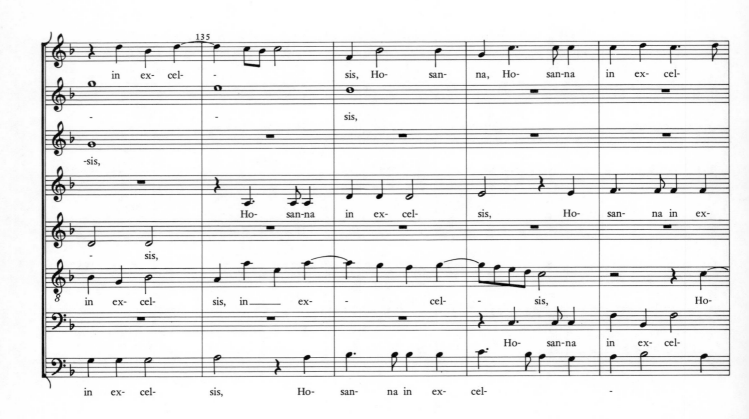

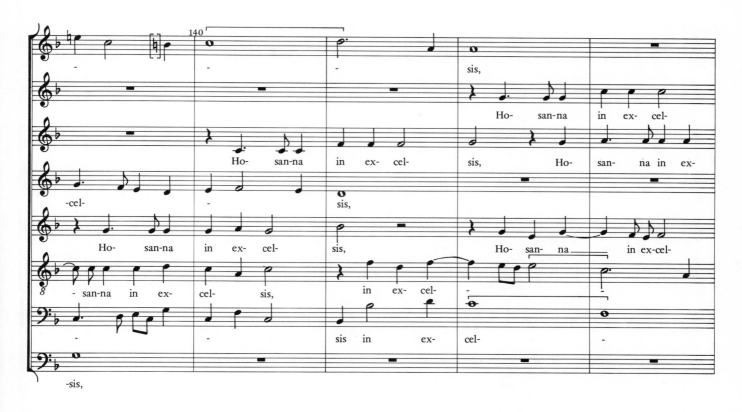

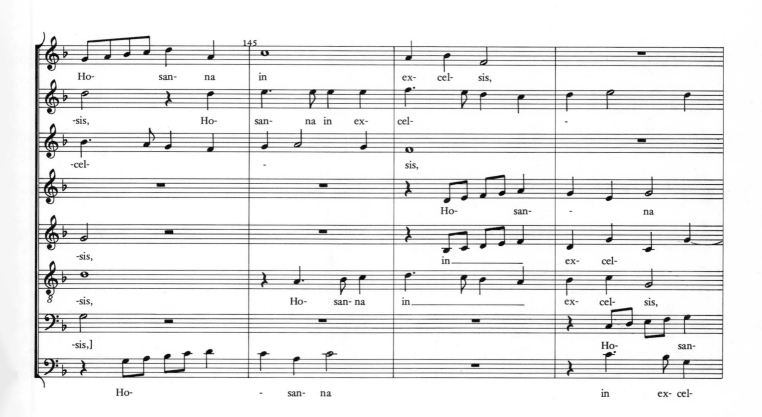

Agnus Dei